For Marrin & Evan ~ for family!

ONE LUCKY GIRL

George Ella Lyon

2/2000

by George Ella Lyon ❧ illustrated by Irene Trivas

Ink

DORLING KINDERSLEY PUBLISHING, INC.

A Richard Jackson Book

Dorling Kindersley Publishing, Inc., 95 Madison Avenue, New York, New York 10016
Visit us on the World Wide Web at http://www.dk.com

Dorling Kindersley books are available at special discounts for bulk purchases for sales promotions
or premiums. Special editions, including personalized covers, excerpts of existing guides, and corporate imprints
can be created in large quantities for specific needs. For more information, contact Special Markets Dept.,
Dorling Kindersley Publishing, Inc., 95 Madison Avenue, New York, New York 10016; fax: (800) 600-9098.

Library of Congress Cataloging-in-Publication Data
Lyon, George Ella
One lucky girl / by George Ella Lyon ; illustrated by Irene Trivas. — 1st ed.
p.   cm.
Summary: Even though their trailer is destroyed by a tornado,
a young boy's family is grateful because they find his baby sister alive.
ISBN 0-7894-2613-7
[1. Tornadoes—Fiction.   2. Family life—Fiction.]   I. Trivas, Irene, ill.   II. Title.
PZ7.L9954On   2000   [E]—dc21   98-41149   CIP   AC

Book design by Jennifer Browne. The illustrations for this book were created with pastels.
The text of this book is set in 18 point Book Antiqua. Printed and bound in U.S.A.

First Edition, 2000
2   4   6   8   10   9   7   5   3   1

For Steve, who was there,
and for Mary Jean,
an all-weather friend.
—G.E.L.

To Frosty
—I.T.

Becky's baby summer, we lived
in a trailer at the racetrack.
Dad was a jockey,
Mom walked horses,
and I played baseball
in the field across from the barns.

No matter how bright the sun,
how high the ball,
I was there to catch it.
Hawkeye, Dad called me.

One Sunday, about four o'clock,
Mom and Dad were sitting in the shade.
I was oiling my glove.
Becky was down for a nap
in her crib in the trailer.
"Sky looks funny," I said.

Right then it got sick quiet—
no breeze, no bird cry.
I could see a black finger of wind
twisting toward us.
"Tornado!" somebody yelled.
We hit the dirt.

The world went dark, and it sounded like
we were under a stampede of horses.
In the roar I could hear metal being torn apart.

Then it was over.
We all got to our feet.
Mom's cheek was cut.
I still had the glove on my hand.

The Pooles' trailer lay on its side;
the Higgins's was upside down.

It took a minute to realize ours was gone.

All the screams nobody had screamed
tore out of my mother's mouth.
She ran to the frame and wheels—all that was left.
"Becky!" she hollered into the sky.

Mr. Higgins called back, "Are you okay?"
"It's Becky," I said.
"We've got to find her!"

Parts of our trailer
made a line across the field
like a road of crumpled tinfoil.

"That way!" Dad said, and took off running.
Mom, Mr. Higgins, and I were right behind.

At the first piece of siding
they stopped to search.
"Be careful!" Mom cried
as they lifted it to look under.

I held my breath,
but Becky wasn't there.

They did the same thing
with a piece of roof.

The third time they stopped,
I ran on
toward the training track.
I thought I saw something.

I reached the fence
and could see in the dirt
a skillet and a doorknob,
but out in the middle . . . on the grass . . .
what was that?

It looked like—I got through the fence
and was running, gulping air—
it couldn't be, but it looked like—

a dream, the best you could ever have,
the one where you find your treasure.

Right there in the green grass,
plain as cake on a plate

stood Becky's crib—
my heart did a flip—
with Becky still inside it.

"She's here!" I hollered.
"Mom! Dad! She's here!"

And Becky, who had just slept through
the wildest ride of her life,
woke up squalling.
"Yahoo!" I yelled, and jumped for the sky.

And then we were laughing and hugging and crying,
and Mr. Higgins took off shouting.
In a few minutes neighbors gathered.

"I came as soon as I counted my kids,"
Mrs. Fernandez said. "That's one amazing baby
you got. One lucky girl."

"A miracle," Mr. Poole declared.
"How did you find her?"

"We were looking in the ruins,"
Mom said, all smiles and tears.
"It was Nick who found her."

"Hawkeye," Dad said.
There were tears on his face, too.

"But where are we going to live?" I asked.

Dad put one arm around me,
the other around Mom and Becky.
"Together," he said.